First published 1990 by Walker Books Ltd
87 Vauxhall Walk, London SE11 5HJ

This edition produced for
The Book People Ltd, Hall Wood Avenue
Haydock, St Helens WA11 9UL

Printed in Hong Kong

ISBN 0-7445-1380-4

SILAS
THE
OWL

Kate Petty · Shona Grant

TED SMART

Silas was the last of the baby barn owls to hatch. It was a good mouse year and there was plenty of food for all four owlets.

Silas was still only a ball of fluff
when the other owlets were sprouting
proper feathers; even big owls keep some
fluffy feathers to help them fly silently.

Silas watched the father owl drift
noiselessly into the night air, his elegant
wings spread wide. No mouse – nor vole,
nor shrew – would hear his approach
until it was too late.

At first, Silas's downy little
wings weren't much use for flying.
He crouched down, knees knocking
in fright, trying so hard to be silent
that he couldn't always be found.

Before long, Silas was feathered in white and gold. A beautiful heart-shaped ruff framed his face. And he was a good hunter. Silently he flew back and forth across the fields searching for tiny prey. Silently he swooped down on his victims.

Silas ate his food in his favourite elm tree.
The ground below was littered with owl pellets.
"Must be an owl round here," people said.
Silas turned his head right round
to look at them.

Silas didn't think much of people. But he enjoyed frightening them as he glided like a ghost across the graveyard and then let out his unearthly shriek. "Eeeeeeeeek!"

When snow hid the creatures on the ground, Silas often had to hunt right through the day. He needed a warmer resting place, but the barn was newly repaired and he couldn't squeeze in.

Silas couldn't believe his eyes. The farmer was making a hole for him. "Wouldn't mind some barn owls," he told the children. "Stop the mice from eating our hay."

Silas made the barn his new home.

He found a female barn owl to share it with him.
Three of their eggs have hatched. Silas can't wait to
see the fourth.

Topsy + Tim

have a birthday party

Jean and Gareth Adamson

Blackie

British Library Cataloguing in Publication Data
Adamson, Jean, 1928–
Topsy and Tim have a birthday party
I. Title   II. Adamson, Gareth, 1925–1982
823'.914[J]   PZ7

ISBN 0-216-92599-1
ISBN 0-216-92598-3 Pbk

Blackie and Son Limited
7 Leicester Place
London WC2H 7BP

Printed in Portugal

It was Topsy and Tim's birthday.
The first thing they saw when
they woke up was a pile of
birthday presents.

The postman brought them lots of
birthday cards and a package
from Granny.

'Happy birthday, twins,' he said.
'How did you know it was
our birthday?' asked Topsy.
'I guessed!' laughed the postman.

After breakfast, Topsy and Tim
went into the garden to try out
their new roller skates.

'Happy birthday, Topsy and Tim,'
shouted their friends over the fence.
'How did you know it was our
birthday?' asked Tim.
'Because you've invited us to your
party this afternoon, silly,'
said Stevie Dunton.

Later, Dad took them to the shops to buy party balloons and candles for their birthday cake.

'Happy birthday, Topsy and Tim,'
said Mrs Patel.
'How did you know it was our birthday?'
asked Topsy and Tim.
'A little bird told me,' said Mrs Patel.

When they got home, Topsy and Tim
helped to get everything ready
for their birthday party. Dad
showed them how to blow up the balloons.

Then they hung the balloons
in bright bunches round the room.

Topsy and Tim and Dad went into
the kitchen to help make the
party tea. Mummy showed Topsy
how to ice the little cakes.
Tim stuck a sweet on top of
each one.

Dad was putting sticks into the party sausages. He popped a sausage into his mouth, then gave one each to Topsy and Tim.
'Stop that,' said Mummy, 'or there won't be any left for the party.'

'Can Tim and I put the candles
on our birthday cake?' asked Topsy.
'No,' said Mummy. 'You're having
a surprise birthday cake, so
I'll put the candles on. You can
help Dad put the food on the tea table.'

Topsy and Tim enjoyed carrying the
wibbly wobbly jellies.

Everything was ready for the party.
Then their friends began to arrive.
Vinda was the first, then Tony Welch.
Stevie Dunton and Andy Anderson
came together. 'Here I am,' said Kerry.
Rai was just behind.

They had all brought birthday presents
for Topsy and Tim.
'Is everyone here?' asked Mummy.
'Everyone except Josie,' said Topsy.
'We can't start without Josie,' said Tim.
'I think we'd better,' said Mummy.

First they played Musical Chairs.
Dad played the music. Each time
the music stopped, they had to
find a chair to sit on.
'I've not got a chair,' said Topsy.
'You're out, then,' said Dad.
Stevie Dunton won Musical Chairs.
Mummy gave him a prize.

Next they played Oranges and Lemons.
Mummy and Dad made the arch and sang
'Oranges and lemons, say the bells
of St Clement's . . .'

'Time for one more game before tea,'
said Mummy. 'We'll play Pass the Parcel.'
Just then, the doorbell rang.
It was Josie Miller.
'Hooray,' said Topsy and Tim.

Josie sat down between Topsy and
Tim and the music began. Every time
the music stopped, the one holding
the parcel had to unwrap it a bit more.
'Everybody's won something except me,'
grumbled Josie. Then she won
Pass the Parcel. 'This is a good party,'
said Josie.

'Time for the birthday tea,' said Dad.
There was plenty of food for
everyone and lots of orange
to drink.
'I *was* thirsty,' said Andy Anderson.

Mummy came in with the surprise
birthday cake. 'Ooh, it's a dinosaur!'
said the children.
The dinosaur had candles all down
its back.

All the children sang 'Happy Birthday' and Topsy and Tim blew out their birthday candles with one big puff.